RONAN

MATHS AND PHYSICS EXPERT

TEAM MEDIC

THE GLOBAL HEROES ARE A GROUP OF CHILDREN FROM AROUND THE WORLD, RECRUITED BY THE MYSTERIOUS BILLIONAIRE, MASON ASH. FROM THE BEEHIVE, THEIR TOP SECRET ISLAND HEADQUARTERS, THEY USE THEIR SPECIAL SKILLS TO HELP PROTECT THE FUTURE OF THE EARTH AND EVERYTHING THAT LIVES ON IT.

For Vicky, with Love T.M.D. always
Damian

FRANKLIN WATTS

First published in Great Britain in 2022 by Franklin Watts

1 3 5 7 9 10 8 6 4 2

Author: Damian Harvey
Illustrator: Alex Paterson
Series Editor: Melanie Palmer
Design: Lisa Peacock

A CIP catalogue record for this book
is available from the British Library.

ISBN 978 1 4451 8298 8 (pbk)
ISBN 978 1 4451 8635 1 (ebook)

Printed and bound in Great Britain by Clays Ltd, St Ives plc

The paper and board used in this book are made from wood from responsible sources.

Franklin Watts
An imprint of
Hachette Children's Group
Part of Hodder and Stoughton
Carmelite House
50 Victoria Embankment
London EC4Y 0DZ

An Hachette UK Company
www.hachette.co.uk
www.hachettechildrens.co.uk

CONTENTS

1. LITTER DROP   7

2. THE FLOATING ISLAND   21

3. ON THE BEACH   35

4. A SIGHTING   49

5. SHIP HUNTING   63

6. RIVERS OF RUBBISH   75

7. CAPTAIN RANSOM   89

8. COLLISION COURSE   101

FACT FILES   114

QUIZ   122

GLOSSARY   124

CHAPTER ONE
LiTTER DROP

High above the jungle floor, a gentle breeze blew across the roof of the Beehive, the Global Heroes' top secret headquarters. Mo's crisp packet blew off his table and scuttled across the floor.

He watched with interest as the breeze swept it past Ling's chair and towards the railings at the edge of the roof. It was almost as if it had a life of its own.

When she saw it, Ling leapt out of her chair and ran after it. She had only taken a few steps when the breeze carried the wrapper through the railings and out of sight.

"Look at it go," laughed Mo. "You're too slow."

"Go and pick that up," Ling snapped.

"You're joking, aren't you?" said Mo. "It was only a crisp packet."

"Only a crisp packet!" cried Ling. "Go and get it."

"But I don't know where it landed," said Mo, peering over the railings. "Anyway, how much harm can one crisp packet do?"

"Crisp packets and other plastic wrappers don't just disappear, you know," said Ling. "It could lie in the ground for one hundred years or more."

Mo looked surprised. "That's a really long time," he said.

"Yes, it is," said Ling. "And there's a good chance that a bird or some other creature will try and eat it."

"I never thought of that," Mo admitted,

starting to feel guilty. He knew if an animal ate a wrapper it would make it very poorly. Ling began talking about what it would be like if everyone dropped a single wrapper onto the floor. As she did, Mo quietly made his way towards the stairs. He had already decided what he

was going to do. Down on the ground,
Mo rooted around in the plants and
bushes until he finally spotted the crisp
packet.

He waved it in the air to show that
he had found it. High above, Ling waved
at him from the roof.

Mo stuffed the crisp packet into his pocket and made a note to never leave even a single wrapper lying around ever again. Just then, the Beehive's alarm began sounding, calling the Global Heroes to the control pod. Stepping back inside, he couldn't help wondering what the emergency might be this time.

★ ★ ★

On the huge television screen in the control pod, Mason Ash sat behind his desk, his face hidden in the shadows as always.

"Good morning, everyone," he said. "I hope you're rested after your last mission, because the world needs your help."

"We're ready," said Fernanda, excitedly.

"What is it today I wonder?" asked Ronan.

On the screen they saw huge waves washing up onto a beach. It should have been a beautiful sight, but the water was full of rubbish.

"This beach is near Rio de Janeiro, in Brazil," said Professor Darwin.

Fernanda gasped. "I went there when I was little," she said.

"Yuk!" said Ronan. "Why would

anyone go there?"

"Because it's beautiful," said
Fernanda. "I mean … it *was* beautiful.

"What's happened?"

"The beach has been swamped by
a tidal wave of plastic," Mason Ash told
them.

"It looks horrible," said Keira.

"It's dangerous too," the professor
told them. "It harms the wildlife and it's
hazardous to humans. Fish can swallow
tiny bits of plastic and then humans eat
the fish."

Mason Ash told them their mission
was to find out where the waste had
come from and to find out what could be

done about it.

"Who is going on this mission?" asked Fernanda.

"Your medical knowledge could come in useful," Mason told her. "And I think Ling's knowledge of environmental issues will be important, too. You'll also need to take some additional equipment with you so you'll need both eco-boosters. Mason said that he wanted Ronan to take the second eco-booster as his scientific, logical approach to things could be a big help, too.

"What about me and Keira?" asked Mo. "What can we do?"

Mason explained that Keira would

be able to put her technical skills to good use from the Beehive. Mo would be providing essential support by gathering important data and doing research along the way.

"Come on then." said Fernanda. "We'd better go and get ready."
While Mason spoke to the team, Professor Darwin went to prepare the eco-boosters – the Global Heroes eco-friendly aircraft. Ling and Fernanda were taking one and Ronan would be taking the other. That left Mo and Keira to provide support from The Beehive.

"There's just one more thing," said Mason, as they were about to leave.

"Make sure you keep your eyes open and your wits about you. I have a feeling you won't be alone out there."

"Don't tell me," said Fernanda. "Evilooters!"

"Yes!" Mason replied. "Wherever there's an ecological disaster, you're sure to find those criminals are involved in one way or another."

* * *

Mo couldn't help feeling envious as Fernanda, Ling and Ronan climbed into their eco-boosters. He knew supporting them from the Beehive was important, but it didn't feel as exciting as actually going.

As the two eco-boosters took off, Keira turned to Mo. "Come on," she said. "Let's get to the control pod."

"Okay," said Mo, still unhappy about staying in the base.

"We've got donuts," said Keira, with a smile.

"Donuts!" said Mo. "Why didn't you say so. Staying here might not be so bad after all."

Professor Darwin had programmed the eco-boosters to carry them across the ocean to the coast of Brazil. Flying on autopilot meant there was nothing to do but sit back and relax.

CHAPTER TWO
THE FLOATING ISLAND

Fernanda closed her eyes and thought about the mission. The sight of all of that rubbish on the beach had shocked her. It was hard to imagine why anyone would do such a thing. Mason Ash said their mission was to find out where the waste had come from and see what could be done about it.

Back at the Beehive, Keira was following their progress on her GPS tracker, and Mo was seeing what information he could unearth about plastic waste. When the eco-booster's radio came to life, Fernanda guessed it was them. But instead, it was Professor Darwin's voice she heard.

"We've had reports of something interesting," the professor said. "I've just altered your course slightly so you can take a look."

"What is it, Professor?" asked Ronan from his eco-booster.

"We're not sure," the professor replied. "The pilot that spotted it was flying too high to be certain. Just keep your eyes open for anything unusual."

Through the eco-booster's canopy, the deep blue of the Atlantic Ocean stretched out before them, but there was no sign of anything else. Then Ling pointed at something off to one side.

"What's that?" she asked.

Fernanda looked where her friend
was pointing. "It's just an island," she said.

"But there are no islands near here,"
replied Ling. "Look at the map."

Fernanda frowned at the navigation screen in front of them. Ling was right. There were no islands in that area. But if it wasn't as island … what on earth was it? There was only one way to find out.

"I'm going to take us down for a closer look," said Fernanda.

"Okay," replied Professor Darwin. "But be careful."

Fernanda took control of the eco-booster and gently eased the steering column forwards. The craft gradually lost height until they were flying just a few metres above the waves. From there, it was clear that the island wasn't an island at all.

"It's all rubbish," cried Ling. "It looks like a floating garbage patch."

"We had a feeling that's what you'd find," said Mo.

Mo had just been reading about floating garbage patches in the oceans. He explained that plastic and other rubbish gets dumped or washed out to sea, then the current makes it collect in huge patches like the one they were looking at.

"It poisons the water and it damages life in the ocean," he added. "Some creatures eat it and some get

caught in it. Whichever happens, it's not good for the creatures."

Mo told them that work was being done to clear up the floating garbage patches, but the one they were looking at seemed to be new. "It's not on any of the reports I've read," he said.

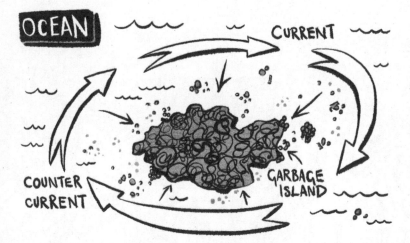

"Then we need to find out where this has come from," said Ling.

As the eco-boosters flew over the garbage patch, she took photographs to send back to the Beehive. Then Ronan spotted something else.

"Ship ahoy!" he called.

Just beyond the floating garbage patch was a large ship sailing away from the garbage patch. As it cut through the waves, thick black smoke belched from its chimneys.

"I can see it on our GPS tracker," said Keira. "It looks like it's heading towards Brazil."

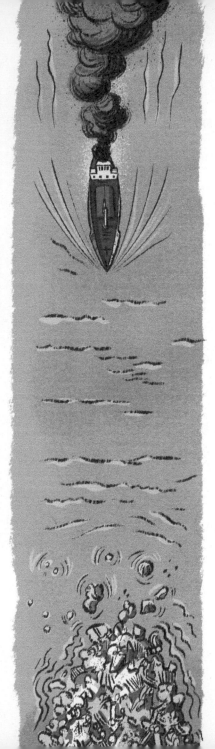

"Look at all that air poisoning pollution," said Fernanda.

"And look at all that fuel leaking into the ocean behind it," said Ling. "It's poisoning the sea and it's deadly for sea creatures." The two eco-boosters sped up as they followed the ship.

"Don't get too close," warned Professor Darwin. "We don't know who they are."

"I just want to take a picture," said Fernanda.

Flying past, they could see that the ship was very old. Paint was peeling from its hull and there was rust everywhere. On the deck, some of the crew stood watching them. One of them, a man with a grubby white hat and a long beard, held a telescope to his eye.

"I bet he's the captain," said Fernanda.

"And I bet he knows something about all of that floating waste," said

Ronan.

Ling snapped away with her camera, determined to get as many pictures as she could.

"Try to get the ship's name," said Mo. "That'll make it easier for us to trace."

"It's called *The Armless Octopus*," said Ronan. "I won't forget that name in a hurry."

Leaving the ship behind, the eco-boosters continued towards the coast of Brazil. It wasn't long before Rio De Janeiro with its tall buildings and huge statue came into sight.

Instead of heading for the city,

the two craft came in to land on what appeared to be a pebble beach lined with palm trees. It wasn't until they clambered out of their eco-boosters that they realised the mistake they had made.

CHAPTER THREE
ON THE BEACH

The beach was covered with rubbish.
Plastic bags, crates, footballs, fishing nets,
broken toys, cups, cartons and all sorts
of other junk stretched as far as the eye

could see.

"It looks even worse now we're here," said Fernanda.

"It smells worse too," said Ronan, covering his nose.

"But where has it come from?" asked Fernanda.

Ling spotted a group of people further along the beach, collecting rubbish and putting it into sacks. "Perhaps they can help us," she said.

"And we could help them," said Fernanda, eager to join in.

"Wait!" said Ronan, getting something from his eco-booster. "We should put these on first."

He handed Ling and Fernanda a pair of gloves and a face mask. "We don't know what we're going to come across."

When they reached the litter pickers, Ronan asked why some of them only picked up plastic bottles, while others collected tin cans or fishing nets and rope.

"Separating the waste makes it easier to recycle," said one of the litter pickers. "Things that can't be recycled get put into landfills, like giant holes in the ground."

"That's a lot of waste," said Ronan.

"And most of it is single use plastic," said Ling. "Things like bottles that people use once, then throw away."

The three friends discovered that the litter pickers were volunteers who came to the beach every day. Their task had recently got much harder, thanks to the wave of garbage.

Helping pick up the rubbish, the team quickly realised how important the gloves and masks were. As well as rubbish, the beach was littered with dead fish and other creatures.

They learnt that some rubbish, like fishing nets or rope, often got washed into the sea from passing boats. Most of the other waste had come from further up the coast.

"Then that's where we need to go," said Ronan.

Reluctantly leaving the volunteers to continue their work, the three friends headed back to their eco-boosters.

★ ★ ★

As they flew further up the country another call came in from the Beehive. "Hey guys," said Mo. "Guess what we've discovered?"

But before any of them had chance to have a guess, Keira joined in. "Remember that ship?" she said.

"You mean *The Armless Octopus!*" replied Ronan.

"That's it," said Mo. "It was stolen from a scrap yard a few months ago."

"Stolen!" said Fernanda. "But why would anyone want to steal a wreck of a ship like that?"

"That's a good question," agreed Mo. "But we don't know the answer to that yet. Perhaps you can find out."

"Tidal waves of waste!" said Ling. "This is

all starting to sound a bit fishy to me."

"I bet they're all connected in some way," said Fernanda.

"You might be right," said Keira. "But you're going to have to find proof. As the eco-boosters dropped down through the clouds, the friends got their first view of the Amazon River.

They could see it weaving its way across
the country like a giant snake.

"It's huge," said Ling.

"It's the biggest river in Brazil,"
said Fernanda, proudly. "And the second
biggest in the world."

The two craft came in to land at the edge of a large town, close to the river. From where they were they could see a couple of small boats bobbing around in the water. Further out, larger ships were passing by. Some heading into port and others out to sea.

Clambering out of her eco-booster, Ling noticed a boy standing in one of the little boats.

"I'm going to see what he's doing," she said. "He might be able to help us."

The boy was holding a long pole with a net on the end. Ling thought he was looking for fish, but soon realised it was something else he was trying to catch. She watched as the boy scooped up a plastic bottle and dropped it into the bottom of his boat.

When he saw Ling he gave a friendly wave. "Nice planes," he said.

"They're called eco-boosters," said Ling. "You can have a look if you like."

"Cool!" said the boy, and began paddling his boat towards her. As soon as it touched the riverbank, the boy leapt out and dragged it ashore.

He added his catch of bottles to a sack that he had left leaning against one of the trees. Ling guessed he'd had a busy day as there were two more full sacks close by.

"That's a lot of rubbish," said Ling.

"That is nothing," said the boy. "You should see what it is like in the town."

"That might be useful," thought Ling. "Will you show us?" she asked.

The boy thought for a moment and then grinned. "Sure, if you help carry my bottles," he said.

"It's a deal," said Ling, picking up one of the sacks.

CHAPTER FOUR
A SIGHTING

As they walked back towards the eco-
boosters Ling learned that the boy was
eight years old and his name was Sergio.

"Mother says it means protector or guardian," he said, proudly.

Ling smiled. "Are you protecting the river from all the rubbish?" she asked.

Sergio shrugged. "I am doing it to earn money," he said. "If I do not get money my family cannot eat."

"You mean you get paid for collecting bottles?" said Ling.

Sergio nodded. "Of course," he said. "The collection place gives me a few pennies for them. If I get enough, we can buy some food."

Just then, Ronan came down to join them. "Shall I get one?" he said, pointing

to one of the other sacks of bottles.
Suddenly, Sergio stopped walking and
looked at Ling and Ronan suspiciously.
"You aren't trying to steal my bottles are
you?" he asked.

Ronan shook his head. "No!" he said. "We'd never do that. I just wanted to help."

The boy seemed reassured by this and smiled again. "Sometimes other children try to steal the bottles I have collected," he said. "It is easier than collecting their own."

★ ★ ★

While Ling and Ronan were talking
to Sergio, Fernanda had been busy
looking at one of the large ships on
the river. Without taking her eyes off
it, she reached into her rucksack for
her binoculars and held them up to her
face. "I knew it," she said. "*The Armless
Octopus!*"

Still staring at the ship, Fernanda grabbed the eco-booster's radio and began telling Keira what she'd seen. She was still busy talking when Ling and Ronan arrived with Sergio.

"Thanks, Keira," she said. "We'll set off right away."

"Where are you going?" asked Ling.

"You mean, where are we going," replied Fernanda. She quickly told them about seeing *The Armless Octopus* sailing up the river.

"I told Keira we'd go find out where it's going," she said.

"But Sergio is going to show us all the rubbish in town," said Ling.

Ronan nodded. "It sounds important for our mission," he said.

"You're right," agreed Fernanda. "But I think the ship is important too. Why don't you go with Sergio and I'll follow the ship."

"We can use our radios to keep in touch with you," said Ling.

"Good idea," said Ronan. "I'll get our rucksacks."

Ronan grabbed two rucksacks from his eco-booster and handed one to Ling.

Once their radios were switched on, they
slung the rucksacks onto their backs.
"Let's get going," said Ling, picking up
one of the sacks of bottles.

"We'll meet you back here at the landing zone."

"I'll let you know if I see anything interesting," said Fernanda, speaking into her radio.

Ronan rolled his eyes. "Thanks, Fernanda. But I can hear you from here without your radio."

"I just wanted to test it," Fernanda replied. "You know … just in case."

They watched as Fernanda got into the eco-booster and fastened her safety belt. She gave a thumbs up then started the craft's engines.

As Ling and Ronan followed Sergio, Fernanda's eco-booster rose into the air and flew off over the trees above them. Sergio stopped to watch it for a moment. "I would love to fly in one of those," he said.

"Perhaps one day you will," said Ling. "How far is it to town?"

"Not far now," Sergio replied. "Look, it's just through these trees."

Ling and Ronan were surprised by what they saw. They had expected something like Rio de Janeiro with it's tall, modern buildings. But the buildings here looked very old. Some were concrete while others seemed to be made of wood and bits of junk.

As they walked, Ling and Ronan understood what Sergio had meant about the rubbish. Street corners were piled high with bin bags. Heaps of cardboard lay stacked against walls, and plastic bottles and other rubbish lay at the side of the road.

"It is not always like this," said Sergio. "Sometimes it is better. Sometimes it is worse."

Ling had stopped to take photographs when an awful smell grabbed her attention.

"What is that?" she asked.

Ronan looked over the side of the bridge they were crossing.

"I think it's that," he said.

Ling pulled a face. Instead of water, the bridge stretched over a river of rubbish. There were bottles, cans, plastic bags and even an old fridge.

Along the far side stood a row of buildings with crumbling balconies.

It looked as if they could collapse at any moment.

"That is where I live," said Sergio, pointing at one of the houses. "Now you must wait here … I have something to show you."

CHAPTER FIVE
SHIP HUNTING

Fernanda was sure the ship and the
floating garbage patch were connected.
Hopefully, finding the ship would help the
Global Heroes prove it.

She pulled the steering column towards her and sent the eco-booster soaring high into the air. Far below, the Amazon River stretched away into the distance. From this height, the ships looked like toys and it was hard to tell them apart. Luckily, *The Armless Octopus*, with its chimneys belching thick, black smoke, stood out for miles.

She was about to go after it when Keira's voice came through the radio headset.

"Professor Darwin thinks it would be safest if you kept out of sight of the ship," she said. "The captain and crew have already seen the eco-boosters once.

They might get suspicious if they see them again."

"Good thinking!" Fernanda replied. "That should be simple enough. At least I know which way they're heading."

"According to our satellite images there's a large port further up the river," said Keira. "From what I've read about it, lots of the bigger ships call in there," said Mo. "Perhaps The Armless Octopus will too."

"That's great! Thanks, both of you," Fernanda replied. "Hopefully that's where they're heading then. I'll try and catch up with it there. Can you find out if there's anywhere for me to land when I get there?"

"Will do," replied Mo. "I'll get onto it now."

Fernanda took the eco-booster down, so it was just a little way above the surface of the water.

The downdraught from the engines sent ripples chasing each other towards the shore. Once she was at the right altitude, she gripped the steering column tightly and concentrated on flying. She did not want to let the ship get too far away.

Rounding a bend in the river, Fernanda hoped she might catch sight of it. But, instead, there was a small village made up of wooden houses that stood above the water on stilts. A handful of small fishing boats were moored there, but there was no sign of *The Armless Octopus*.

Fernanda flew on for a while without seeing anything else of interest. She was beginning to wonder how much further she would have to go when the port came into view.

The river was busy here and ships of all shapes and sizes were heading in and out of the docks, but there was no sign of the one she was after.

"I've reached the docks but there's no sign of *The Armless Octopus*," said Fernanda. "I'll need to land and take a closer look."

"We've just found somewhere for you," said Mo. "Well … Mason Ash has."

"He knows someone that owns one of the private docks," said Keira. "Professor Darwin has set a course for you, so you can sit back and have a rest for a minute."

Fernanda grinned and let go of the
steering column to let the autopilot take
control. *Mason knows people all over the
world*, she thought. *It's hardly surprising that
he knows someone here, too.*

★★★

As the eco booster gently touched down,
Fernanda looked around at the private
dock. There were a few little boats
moored there but most of the space was

taken up by a pair of large, expensive-looking yachts.

Fernanda grabbed her rucksack and stepped down from her craft just in time to be greeted by a woman with long dark hair and a friendly smile.

"Welcome," said the woman. "I am Maria Santos. It is so good to finally meet one of the Global Heroes in person."

"You've heard of us?" said Fernanda, sounding surprised.

"Of course," Maria replied. "He tells us about your adventures whenever he passes this way. He is very proud of you all."

Fernanda could feel her face flushing with a mixture of pride and embarrassment.

"Now!" said Maria, clapping her hands. "I know you don't have much time, so how can I help?"

Fernanda showed Maria a photo

of *The Armless Octopus* and told her what they had found out.

Maria shook her head sadly. "I'm afraid I haven't seen a ship like that," she said. "But that is not surprising. A stolen vessel is not one that would come to us. It sounds like these people are up to no good."

Maria showed Fernanda a map of the docks and pointed out a couple of locations that might be worth a look.

"Your eco-booster will be safe here," she said. "But you need to be careful. I do not think these people will be happy if they find you poking your nose into their business."

Fernanda remembered seeing the captain and crew of *The Armless Octopus*, and shuddered. This mission was suddenly starting to feel very scary.

CHAPTER SIX
RIVERS OF RUBBISH

Ling and Ronan were just starting to wonder if Sergio was ever going to return when he came running round the corner waving something in his hand.

"Look! Look!" he said, showing them an old photograph. "This is here." The picture was of a group of young children playing by a river. Some were swimming in the water while others stood on the bank. One boy was in mid-air, caught by the camera as he jumped in.

"That one is my father," said Sergio, pointing at the boy.

"It's hard to even recognise the place," said Ronan.

Sergio agreed. "The children used to swim here but now the river has been poisoned and does not even flow."

"So what happens when it rains?" asked Ling.

"Rivers and streams take rainwater out to sea. When it rains, the streets and houses get flooded," said Sergio.

"That's because the drains and rivers are blocked with rubbish," said Ling. "The rainwater cannot drain away. It carries waste along with it and it also carries diseases."

Sergio told them that the people of Brazil were trying to be more careful with their rubbish. But there were so many people, and so little money that it felt like an impossible task. A lot people did not even have anyone to collect their rubbish. That was one reason it ended being piled up on the street.

Ling suddenly realised how that led to another problem. "Of course," she said. "And when there are heavy rains, all this rubbish gets washed into the rivers."

"That's it!" said Ronan. "And eventually it gets washed out to sea." Ling and Ronan looked at each other knowingly. Some parts of the puzzle were falling into place.

The volunteers they had met cleaning the beach near Rio de Janeiro had told them a lot of the rubbish had come from further up the coast. Now they knew why that was happening. What Sergio had shown them was very useful and they couldn't wait to go and share it with Fernanda.

"We should probably head back to our landing zone," said Ronan. "Thanks for showing us all of this."

"Hey!" Sergio cried. "Don't forget our deal. You said you would help carry the bottles."

Ronan grinned. "Don't worry," he said. "We haven't forgotten."

"Lead the way," said Ling. Although Ronan and Ling were eager to return to the landing zone, they were glad they went with Sergio. The collection place was really a plastic recycling plant. One of the people in charge was Sergio's mother.

They learnt that his mother used to collect plastic bottles from a huge dump. After the dump was closed she was given a job at the recycling plant.

"This is a nicer place to work," she told them. "But I do not earn as much money doing this as I could collecting plastic from the dump."

Sergio's mother told them about other ways that people were recycling things to make money.

"But is making money the most important thing?" Ronan asked.

Sergio's mother sighed. "When you cannot afford to feed your family or pay for somewhere to live, then yes," she said. "It becomes more important than recycling, but people are finding ways to do both."

Ling and Ronan listened as Sergio's mother told them about the different things some of her friends and family were doing. They were just about ready to leave when their radios crackled to life.

It was Fernanda.

"You won't believe this," she said. "But I think I've found what's causing all of the pollution problems."

"That's great, Fernanda," Ling replied. "We've found out some causes, too."

"Great," said Fernanda, "but I've found the …"

The radio suddenly went silent.

Ling frowned.

"Fernanda!" she said. "Are you there?"

"Fernanda!" said Ronan, trying his radio.

"Fernanda! Can you hear me? Fernanda!" But there was no reply.

* * *

Fernanda had found *The Armless Octopus* moored at the far side of the port. From her hiding place behind a stack of crates, she could see the captain

watching as a crane dumped a mountain
of plastic waste onto the ship's deck.

With his grubby white hat and long
beard, she had recognised him right away.
He was definitely the person they'd seen
watching them through his telescope as

they had flown past.

The noise from the crane was deafening, but Fernanda didn't mind. Now she had proof that the ship and the plastic waste were connected.

After taking some photographs she called Ling and Ronan to tell them the news. But no sooner had she started to speak than the sound from the crane stopped.

Everything went quiet. Everything except the sound coming from her radio.

Fernanda pressed her hand over the speaker but she could still hear Ronan's muffled voice.

And if she could hear it, that meant the captain of *The Armless Octopus* could probably hear it too.

Sure enough, when she looked back in his direction, she could see him walking towards her hiding place with a curious expression on his face.

CHAPTER SEVEN
CAPTAIN RANSOM

Fernanda closed her eyes and tried
to make herself as small as possible,
hoping that somehow the captain
wouldn't see her.

She could hear the sound of the captain's footsteps getting closer when a man's voice called out, breaking the silence.

"Captain Ransom!" said the man. The captain stopped and scowled.

"That's it for today," the man continued. "I've got your money here."

"There's no need to shout," the captain replied. "We don't need everyone knowing our business."

Fernanda opened her eyes and shifted her position so she could get a look at the other person. It was the crane driver, and he had a large envelope in one hand.

Fernanda quickly took a picture of him
as the man handed the envelope to the
captain.

"You should let everyone know,"
said the crane driver. "You take our plastic

waste away for a very good price. If others did the same we might not have such a huge waste problem here."

The captain took the money and smiled to himself as he headed back to the ship. At the top of the gangplank the crew were waiting eagerly for him. Then, as the crane driver drove off they let out a loud cheer as the captain held the envelope in the air.

"Another pile of money for us," he said. "Now let's go and recycle this pile of junk."

"I thought we were just gonna dump it in the sea," replied one of the crew. "Just like the last lot."

"Of course we're going to dump it in the sea, you fool," cried the captain. "That's how we recycle. Now get this bucket of bolts moving before it sinks."

"Aye, aye, Captain," the crewman replied.

As they prepared to leave, Fernanda watched as the captain leant against the ship's rail and stared down at the dockside as if searching for something. Eventually, he turned and headed inside leaving the crew to their duties.

Fernanda didn't dare move until the ship began to head away from the dock. *That was close,* she thought as she began heading back to her eco-booster.

As she made her way along the dockside, she didn't notice the captain watching her from the bridge through his telescope. And she didn't see the angry look on his face.

Once her eco-booster was in the air, Fernanda called the Beehive to tell the rest of the team everything.

"Captain Ransom's being paid to recycle plastic waste," she said. "But he's just dumping it in the ocean. And now he's leaving with another load."

"We'll let the police know right away," replied Keira. "Hopefully they can

stop the
ship before
it leaves
the river."

As
Fernanda
flew off,
she was so excited that she forgot about
keeping the eco-booster out of sight like
Keira had reminded her to do earlier.
If she'd looked down at *The Armless
Octopus*, she'd have seen Captain Ransom
watching from the bridge.

She might even have seen the angry
look on his face. If there was one thing
Captain Ransom hated, it was interfering

busybodies.

Ronan and Ling were putting on life-jackets when Fernanda reached the landing zone.

"You're just in time," said Ling.

"We're joining some local volunteers cleaning up the river," explained Ronan.

"That sounds great," said Fernanda, grabbing a life-jacket.

The three friends clambered into their dinghy and began paddling away from the shore. As they did, one of the volunteers called over to them.

"Don't go past the green buoys," she said. "Or you'll find yourself dodging the big ships."

"Thanks," Ronan replied. "We'll keep our eyes open."

They hadn't gone far before their dinghy was surrounded by floating rubbish. Fernanda, reached out and picked up a plastic bottle with a long litter picker.

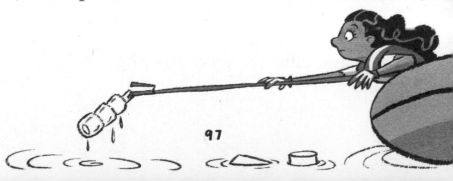

97

"I can't believe that everyone throws their rubbish into the river," she said.

Ronan and Ling began telling her about the things they had discovered on their visit to the town with Sergio. They told her that it wasn't just about people throwing their rubbish into the river. They didn't manage to say much before Fernanda's radio began beeping.

"Hello!" said Fernanda, holding the radio to her mouth.

"Hi guys," said Mo, excitedly. "Guess what?"

"Evilooters," Keira blurted out, before any of them had chance to say anything. "They're who stole the ship.!"

"Captain Ransom isn't even a proper captain," said Mo. "He's wanted by the police in four different countries for his involvement with environmental disasters."

"Make that five countries now," said Fernanda. "He's definitely involved in this disaster too." said Fernanda.

"I knew that the Evilooters would be behind all this somehow," said Ling.

As they were talking, they gradually became aware of a growing noise behind behind them. Ronan looked round and his eyes opened wide with fear. "Ship!" he cried.

EViLOOTER CHARACTERS

CAPTAIN RANSOM

DECEPTION: 88

POLLUTING LEVEL: 70

CUNNING: 75

GREED: 108

ENVIRONMENTAL THREAT: 90

CHAPTER EIGHT
COLLISION COURSE

The river suddenly seemed to be full of boats, all heading in their direction. In the distance, were a group of police launches, but it was the big ship that bothered them the most.

"It's heading right for us," said Ronan.

"It shouldn't even be on this side of the green buoys," said Ling.

"You're right, but we'd better get out of its way," said Ronan, picking up one of the paddles and dipping it into the water.

Ling grabbed the other paddle, but the dinghy didn't want to move. "We're not getting anywhere," she said.

"We must be caught on something," said Ronan.

Fernanda looked over the side and saw what it was right away.

The rope that was used to drag the dinghy ashore had got tangled in an old fishing net.

She pulled on the rope but nothing happened. "It won't budge," she said, pulling on the rope.

The huge ship was getting closer by the second. Its propellers churned up the water and thick black smoke belched from its chimneys as it powered on towards them.

It was then Fernanda recognised it. "It's *The Armless Octopus!*" she cried. Then she realised something else. "They must have seen me flying away from the dock," she said. "That means they know who we are. They're trying to ram us on purpose."

Suddenly, the dinghy lurched forwards as it started to break away from the fishing net that had been holding it back. Ronan and Ling paddled as fast as they could but the ship was gaining on them. It was so close that Fernanda could see Captain Ransom grinning at them.

"It's no use," cried Ronan. "We're not going to make it."

Then, Fernanda saw a surprised look cross Captain Ransom's face. The bow of *The Armless Octopus* rose up in the water and a loud screeching sound filled the air. Just before it reached them the huge ship tilted to one side and came to a grinding halt.

As it did, an avalanche of plastic poured from its deck and into the river.

"It's run aground," said Ronan.

"That was close," said Fernanda.

"If Captain Ransom was a proper captain he'd have known he was heading into shallow water," said Ling.

"He's going to find himself in deep water now," laughed Fernanda. "Here's the police."

"I wouldn't be so sure about that," said Ronan, pointing towards the shore. "They always say rats leave a sinking ship."

Fernanda looked towards the shore, just in time to see Captain Ransom and a handful of his crew clamber up the riverbank before disappearing into the trees.

"We have to do something," said Fernanda. "We can't let him get away."

"We have enough to do," said Ronan. "Look at all that plastic waste."

In the river, the other volunteers had surrounded the floating plastic with their boats and were already busy picking it up. The three friends helped for a while but it was soon time to head back to the landing zone.

When they got there, they were surprised to see Sergio and his mother waiting for them.

"These are for you," said Sergio, handing them a bag.

"Wow, thank you," said Ling, peering inside. "They look fantastic."

"All made from recycled plastic," said Sergio.

"Even the bag," added Mum. "I wanted you to see some of the things the people are doing to get rid of the plastic waste."

Once everything was packed into the eco-boosters they waved goodbye to Sergio and his mum and were soon whizzing over the ocean on their way back to the Beehive.

★ ★ ★

When the eco-boosters touched down, Professor Darwin, Mo and Keira were waiting to greet them. Mason Ash was there, too, speaking to them from the TV screen as usual. "Welcome home," he said. "Now tell us all about it."

Fernanda, Ling and Ronan took turns to tell everyone what they had found out on the mission. Then they showed them the things that Sergio and his mum had given them.

"These collapsible cups can fit into your bag or even your pocket," said Ronan. "They can be used many times."

"And look at these beach shoes," said Ling. "All recycled plastic."

"It's great to see people are able to make a living by recycling some of the plastic," said Mo. "But people need to try and stop using plastic at all."

Keira told them that plastic straws and cups had already been banned in some areas of Brazil, but there was still a long way to go.

"You're right," said Professor Darwin. "It will take time and a lot of effort. "

"It sounds like this mission has been a success," said Mason Ash. "You've found out where the plastic waste comes from and thought about ways to get rid of it."

"And don't forget," said Professor Darwin. "You've also learnt that it's not just villains like the Evilooters that are responsible for the waste. It's normal people too."

"Everyone has a responsibility to look after the planet," said Ling. "Even if it starts with picking up a single wrapper," said Mo, with an embarrassed grin.

THE END

COUNTRY PROFILE:

FAST FACTS:

- Brazil is the largest country in South America and the fifth largest country in the world

- Brazil has a temperate, tropical climate and is home to a large area rainforest as well as huge stretches of coastline which border the Atlantic Ocean

BRAZIL

* The national language is Portuguese

* The capital city is Brasília

BRAZIL

Rio de Janeiro

* The Amazon River, second longest river in the world, runs through the whole country and enters the Atlantic Ocean from Brazil.

FACT SHEET:

Brazil is home to the highest variety of animals in the world. It hosts nearly two thirds of the Amazon rainforest as well as a multitude of sea creatures including turtles and bull sharks.

TURTLE FAST FACTS:

* Turtles don't have teeth – they have mouths like beaks to grab their food

* They lay their eggs on sand

* Turtle shells are made of over 50 bones – so they are extremely hard!

* They eat coral

BULL SHARK FAST FACTS:

* They can live in both salt water and fresh water
* A baby bull shark is called a pup
* They usually eat fish, stingrays and smaller sharks
* They can swim at speeds of up to 40 km/h

Brazil has the largest population and land area in south America. Sadly, around 325,000 metric tonnes of plastic waste from the land enter the oceans each year.

CAUSE:

Waste from the land, such as litter on beaches, gets swept out or dumped at sea. Around 80% of plastic in the sea originates from cities and is carried by the river into the ocean.

EFFECT:

The ocean waves gradually fragment the waste, turning them into tiny microplastics. Around half of all marine turtles have ingested plastic or other human rubbish – mistaking it for food such as jellyfish. Plastic washed up on beaches can also limit space for nesting and block tiny hatchlings' paths to the ocean.

Brazil is leading a campaign to remove all plastic in the wild. And there are many ideas about how to reuse plastic waste:
* Skateboards are being made of plastic bottle caps that are melted and moulded

* Pop–up vending machines for recycling bottles in return for money

FACT SHEET:

Wildife and natural habitats are becoming endangered because of human activity.

It's not too late to help look after the planet.

Little steps can make a big difference … Join the Global Heroes in their mission to protect Earth's future. Here are some ideas, but there are plenty more!

CLIMATE ACTION

1) Carry reusable items with you

2) Avoid the use of disposable cutlery, cups, straws and bags

3) Find out about local community projects such as

– a local litter pick

– collecting rubbish for bottle banks

4) Join a plastic-free movement

5) Try to reuse and recycle as much as you can at home

6) Take rubbish home with you

QUIZ

1) What is the name of the ship that the Global Heroes team pursue?

2) Who is Captain Ransom?

3) What gets entangled with the dinghy?

4) What is Sergio collecting and why?

5) Which river do the team travel down?

6) What do the team see on the ocean before they land in Brazil?

7) Which city do the team visit?

GLOSSARY

AUTOPILOT – a computer that helps steer a vehicle, such as a plane

BUOY – a floating object in water

COLLAPSIBLE – can be folded into a smaller shape

DINGHY – a small boat

DOWNDRAUGHT – the downward movement of air

LANDFILL – a dump where rubbish is taken to be buried in the ground

LIFE JACKET – a float to keep you above water

LITTER PICKER – a long stick-like device to pick up rubbish

LOGICAL – thinking carefully to work something out

PLASTIC – hard-wearing material that takes a long time to break down

POISON – something which causes harm to a living thing

PROPELLERS – rotating blades that turn quickly to help a vehicle to move

RECYCLING PLANT – factory used for recycling materials

STILTS – tall structure to lift something up higher

TELESCOPE – long tube with glass to help see things in the distance

READ
ARCTIC ADVENTURE
TO FIND OUT WHAT MISSION MO, FERNANDA, KEIRA, RONAN AND LING ARE ON NEXT!

GLOBAL HEROES

JOIN THE GLOBAL HEROES TEAM
IN THESE FANTASTIC
ADVENTURES:

9781445180953

9781445182988

9781445182964

9781445182971